**For my dad,
Mr. Christmas
– MF**

**For Blitzen
– CA**

Text copyright © 2016 by Maureen Fergus
Illustrations copyright © 2016 by Cale Atkinson

Tundra Books, an imprint of Penguin Random House Canada Young Readers, a Penguin Random House Company

Library and Archives Canada Cataloguing in Publication

Fergus, Maureen, author
The day Santa stopped believing in Harold / by Maureen Fergus ; illustrated by Cale Atkinson.

Issued in print and electronic formats.
ISBN 978-1-77049-824-2 (bound)

I. Atkinson, Cale, illustrator II. Title.

PS8611.E735D397 2016   jC813'.6   C2015-905764-7

Published simultaneously in the United States of America by Tundra Books of Northern New York, an imprint of Penguin Random House Canada Young Readers, a Penguin Random House Company

Library of Congress Control Number: 2015955125

Acquiring Elf: Tara Walker
Editing Elf: Samantha Swenson
Designing Elf: Kelly Hill
The text was set in Burbank (the font, not California).
The artwork was created in Santa's Workshop with Photoshop.
Printed and bound in China

www.penguinrandomhouse.ca

2   3   4   5   20   19   18   17

tundra | Penguin Random House
TUNDRA BOOKS

THE DAY SANTA STOPPED BELIEVING IN HAROLD

WORDS
BY
**MAUREEN
FERGUS**

ART BY
**CALE
ATKINSON**

tundra

ne stormy night very close to Christmas, Santa and Mrs. Claus were sitting in their cozy little log cabin at the North Pole. Mrs. Claus was busy mending the seam of Santa's fourth best pair of red velvet pants. Santa was *supposed* to be going over the roster for this year's sleigh team. Instead, he was moping.

Several times, Mrs. Claus asked Santa what was wrong. Each time, he muttered, "Nothing" and then sighed loudly.

Finally, Mrs. Claus said, "Papa, I can't help you if you won't tell me what the problem is."

"Alright," said Santa with another sigh. "Well, you know Harold?"

Mrs. Claus smiled. "Brown hair, freckles, lost a tooth last week, sometimes forgets to — "

"Stop!" interrupted Santa in a choked voice. "Don't say another word. You don't need to keep pretending on my account because . . . because . . . I don't believe in Harold anymore."

Mrs. Claus stared at Santa as though he'd suddenly sprouted antlers.

"Look, Harold has always been a big part of my Christmas and I still like the *idea* of Harold," explained Santa. "But lately I've come to realize that there are a lot of things about Harold that just don't make sense."

"Like what?" asked Mrs. Claus.

"For one thing, I'm pretty sure his mom writes his Santa letter," said Santa.

"So what if she does?" said Mrs. Claus. "That doesn't mean anything."

"Maybe not," said Santa. "But what about the snack, huh? What about *that*?"

"What about it?" asked Mrs. Claus.

"I think Harold's *dad* lays out my snack on Christmas Eve," whispered Santa dramatically. "Think about it! Harold is way too small to lift a big carton of milk. He can barely hold his own head up!"

"Papa, Harold isn't a *baby* anymore — "

"Yes, well, that's another thing, isn't it?" said Santa. "That Harold who sat on my knee at the mall last year didn't even *look* like the real Harold!"

"Harold is a real person, Papa," said Mrs. Claus. "Real people look different from year to year."

Santa wasn't listening. "You know what's going on here, don't you?" he asked. "Harold's parents are trying to trick me into believing in him."

"And just *why* would they want to do that?" asked Mrs. Claus.

"They think that if I know the truth about Harold, Christmas will be ruined for me," cried Santa. "Either that, or they want the Harold gifts all for themselves!"

Mrs. Claus shook her head and said, "You know what you're doing, don't you? You're *looking* for reasons not to believe in Harold instead of just accepting him as one of the best, most magical parts of Christmas."

Santa looked uncomfortable — and maybe even a little uncertain. But all he said was, "I know what I know."

The terrible news travelled like a spooked arctic hare. Santa had stopped believing in children!

"Not all children," Santa assured Merpin, the Elf Supervisor in the Computer Gizmo Department.

"Just Harold."

"Uh huh," said Merpin.

"And you know what else?" said Santa. "I'm not the only one who doesn't believe in him. My friends don't believe in him either."

"Uh huh," said Merpin.

"Jack Frost says his mom and dad told him that Harold doesn't exist, and the Abominable Snow Monster says only a baby would believe in Harold."

"Uh huh," said Merpin.

"DO I LOOK LIKE A BABY TO YOU?" boomed Santa.

Merpin stared at Santa's twinkling eyes, rosy cheeks and jiggling jelly belly.

"Forget I asked," sniffed Santa. "I'm going to talk to the reindeer."

The reindeer listened carefully to Santa's evidence against the existence of Harold. Then they whispered among themselves for a few minutes.

Finally, Donner said, "On the one hand, we're not convinced that Harold is real."

"I knew it!" said Santa unhappily.

"On the other hand," continued Donner, "we're not convinced that Harold *isn't* real."

"So what are you saying?" asked Santa.

"What we're saying is that you need *proof*," said Donner. "And we think we know just how you can get it."

Now, strange as it seems, while Santa was up north telling Mrs. Claus and the elves and the reindeer that he didn't think Harold was real, Harold was down south telling his parents and his friends and his turtle that he didn't think Santa was real.

Deep in his heart, Harold *wanted* to believe in Santa, but the older Harold got, the harder it was for him to just have faith.

What I need is proof, thought Harold. *And I think I know just how I can get it.*

That Christmas Eve, Harold hung
his stocking, helped set out the Santa
snack and hugged his parents goodnight
just like he did every Christmas Eve.

On this particular night, however,
after his mom and dad had gone to bed,
Harold tiptoed back into the front room
and hid behind the armchair across from
the fireplace.

If Santa is real, thought Harold drowsily,
I will definitely be able to see him coming.

Many hours later, Santa and the reindeer touched down on the roof of Harold's house, which Santa had saved for last.

Santa's plan was to hide in Harold's front room and see if Harold ran out of his bedroom on Christmas morning. If he did, Santa would know that Harold was real. If he didn't, Harold's parents would have some explaining to do.

After settling into his hiding spot, Santa tried to stay awake,
but it was extremely warm and cozy in Harold's front room,
and Santa was very tired after his hard night's work.
  Slowly, he closed his sleepy eyes.

The next thing Santa knew, it was Christmas morning.

"Too bad we don't know any little boys who'd like to open some presents from Santa," said Harold's mom, who'd spotted Harold hiding behind the armchair.

Aha! thought Santa.

"Too bad there *are* no presents from Santa," whispered Harold's father.

Oops, thought Santa, who'd forgotten
to set out the gifts before hiding.
"I don't care about presents,"
said Harold as he slowly stood up.
"I just wanted to see Santa
. . . and I didn't."
At the sound of Harold's voice,
Santa's heart gave a wild leap.

"YOU'RE REAL!" he shouted joyfully as he jumped up from behind the sofa.

Harold's mother screamed. Harold's
father sprayed coffee everywhere.
    Harold's face lit up like a Christmas tree.
"YOU'RE REAL!" he shouted, running over
to give Santa a hug.

After Harold and Santa got over the shock of finding out that each of them had thought that the other wasn't real, they sat on the floor reading comics, playing with toys and licking candy canes until the sound of tiny hooves impatiently stomping on the roof reminded Santa that it was time to go home.

"Good-bye, Harold! Good-bye Harold's parents!" cried Santa as he prepared to magic himself up the chimney.

"Good-bye, Santa," cried Harold. "See you next Christmas morning!"

"Unless you'd rather fall asleep behind someone else's sofa!" cried his parents.

Santa's big, booming laugh
rang out once, shaking the
walls and knocking several
glass ornaments off the tree.
   And then, in the wink of an eye,
he was gone.

THE END